# Buried Treasure,
## a Pirate's Tale

## Dedicated to the Beautiful Chesapeake Bay

As I write about the Chesapeake Bay, it is my desire to preserve the bay; its inhabitant's stories and environment. Bloodsworth Island inspired the last name for Captain John Bloodsworth. In 1631 William Clayborne and Reverend Richard Jones founded Maryland's first trading settlement on Kent Island. Bloody Point and the lighthouse are still located on the southern shore of Kent Island. Historic London Town, England's first tobacco trading port, is located on the South River as a tourist attraction.

## Acknowledgment

My story's main character, Captain John, is the name I gave to my neighbor's then seven-year-old boy, John Britton, who is adventurous and loves the bay waters.

I appreciate my parents, Louise and Carroll, who encouraged my love of art; my wife, Donna Price Kehne, for her patience; my children Kevin D. Kehne, Kelisa Kehne-Cliff, and their spouses Cindy and CJ.

I thank my wife Donna and Carol Lee Fogler, English instructor, for their editorial reviews. A special thanks goes to Jonna and Marci, Cornell Maritime Press/Tidewater Publishers, for their professional editorial and graphic critiques.

# Buried Treasure,

## a Pirate's Tale

By Carroll Harrison Kehne, Jr.

In the early 1700s, colonists built their settlements on the shores and islands of the Chesapeake Bay, trading goods and treasures transported by English and other foreign ships. Life was difficult for the ships' crews and the colonists. Pirates, also known as picaroons, roamed on the high seas, low bays, and coastal ports. Native American tribes occupied the lands along the bay shores and islands. These pirates and tribes menaced the colonists and crews, often attacking them.

The pirate life was a dangerous choice. Pirates were colorful, daring, and mean men. Most were bloodthirsty, often harsh, wanting only to become rich quick by stealing treasures from others. They loved the dangers, and were fond of rough living and jovial adventures, but many pirates were killed before they could grow old.

Pirates found the new settlers a perfect target of their attacks. Raids on ships sailing into the bay became frequent. It was hard times for ships traveling into the colonial settlements. Virginia and Maryland governors hated the raids. They sent patrol boats to defend the English and colonial vessels. Aye mates, sailing into the Chesapeake Bay was a dangerous trip.

This is a tale of a particularly mean and colorful pirate named Captain John Bloodsworth. He roamed the Chesapeake Bay in the early 1700s and one of his many adventures led him from Smith Island up the Chesapeake Bay.

William Claiborne founded the first English trading settlement in 1631, on Kent Island.

In 1634, St. Mary's City became Maryland's capital. Governor Francis Nicholson moved the capital from St. Mary's City to Annapolis in 1695, and pirates preyed on ships sailing into nearby London Town on the South River to trade for tobacco.

## Chesapeake Bay Map Key

1. Smith Island
2. Burning of British ship
3. Bloodsworth Island
4. James Island
5. London Town
6. Annapolis
7. Burial site of treasure
8. Claiborne settlement
9. Kent Island
10. St. Marys

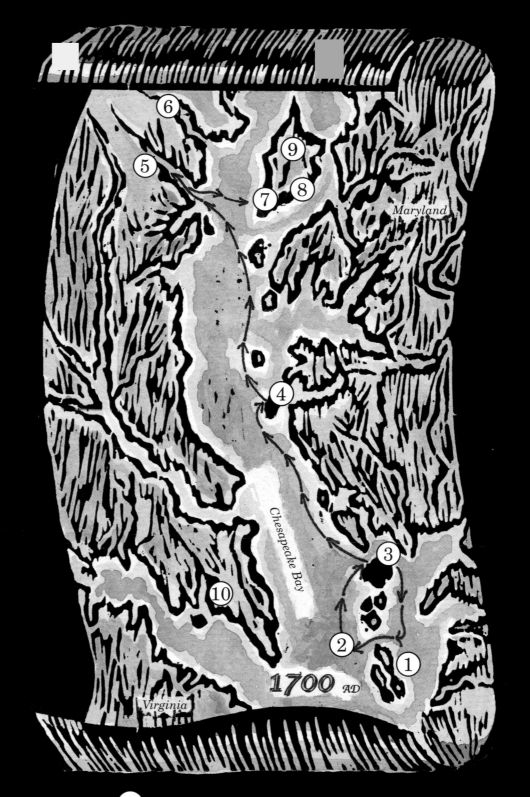

Captain John Bloodsworth is a
vicious, merciless, and daring pirate.
He dresses in bright purple, red, and
gold clothing.

"I love me sparkling jewelry and
polished guns, knives, and swords.
Aye, mates, I'm a good pirate to
boot. Follow me," he announces.

Captain John roams the waters off Smith Island, where many English and Welsh settlers are farmers.

"Shiver me timbers! This be the land of craggy brush, shrubs, and inlets for surprise attacks," he says, "and I often go ashore and take cows for food."

Aargh! The captain enjoys stalking ships!

One day, in the early dawn, the shipmates are in search of ships to plunder.

A lookout in the crow's nest hails, "Ahoy there! An English galley be approaching the starboard bow."

Captain John barks to his pirates, "Aye, aye, mates! Prepare to attack."

The pirates scramble to their posts like wind through the sails.

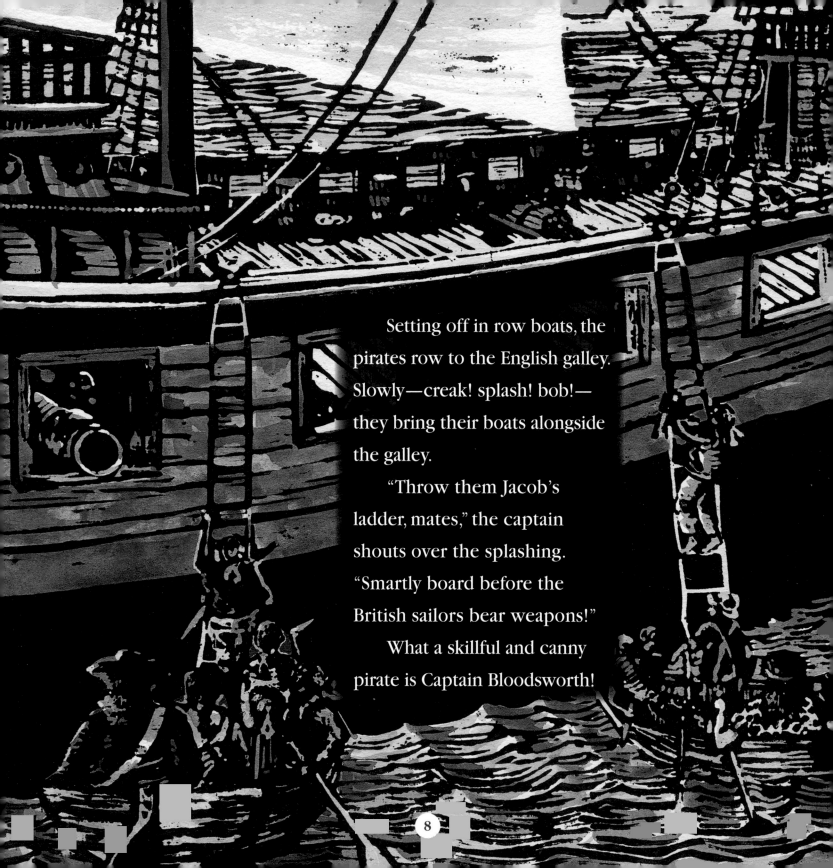

Setting off in row boats, the pirates row to the English galley. Slowly—creak! splash! bob!—they bring their boats alongside the galley.

"Throw them Jacob's ladder, mates," the captain shouts over the splashing. "Smartly board before the British sailors bear weapons!"

What a skillful and canny pirate is Captain Bloodsworth!

As the pirates scramble aboard, like blue crabs in a pot, Captain John hastily commands, "Attack, blow the men down, mates!"

The pirates surprise the English sailors. Hand-to-hand fighting begins with gun, knife, and sword. The pirates shoot, thrust, and wound the ship's crew. The English sailors put up a gallant fight against the savage attack, and soon all are fighting for their lives.

Sneaking around the fading battle, Captain John taunts his latest victim, the English captain. "Good day, captain, welcome to the New World," sneers Captain John.

The pirates' success complete, Captain John leads his men to begin enjoying the spoils of their battle. "Aye, me hearties, let's see what they've got! Secure all on deck!"

The pirates open one full chest of gold and sterling coins. A second chest is full of jewelry and gems.

A happy and pleased Captain John shouts, "Arrr, mates! Remove the prisoners and booty to our ship."

His picaroons remove the chests, barrels of rum, food, and other booty to the pirate ship.

"Burn the galley," yells Captain Bloodsworth, as the plundered English ship wanders empty in the cool bay waters. The blazing red-orange flames rise high in the sky until the ship sinks out of sight.

"Hang a jib to Bloodsworth Island," Captain John commands.

The afternoon air is warm and the water reflects the golden sun.

The pirates lock up the captured men and journey to their island hideout. The waters are calm and a small breeze pushes water lightly against the boat. Swish! Swish! Splash!

"I'm hungry and thirsty," Captain John says.

"Aargh! But ye treasure, Captain," yells a mate. "Where will we bury the treasure?"

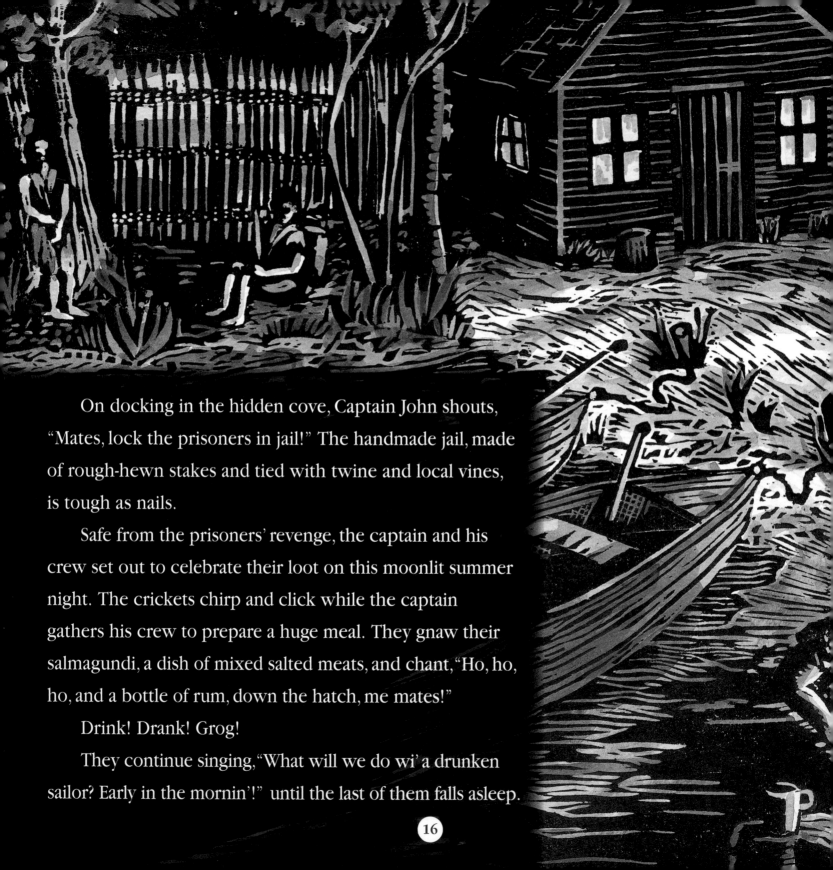

On docking in the hidden cove, Captain John shouts, "Mates, lock the prisoners in jail!" The handmade jail, made of rough-hewn stakes and tied with twine and local vines, is tough as nails.

Safe from the prisoners' revenge, the captain and his crew set out to celebrate their loot on this moonlit summer night. The crickets chirp and click while the captain gathers his crew to prepare a huge meal. They gnaw their salmagundi, a dish of mixed salted meats, and chant, "Ho, ho, ho, and a bottle of rum, down the hatch, me mates!"

Drink! Drank! Grog!

They continue singing, "What will we do wi' a drunken sailor? Early in the mornin'!" until the last of them falls asleep.

Captain Bloodsworth awakes before first light and groggily commands, "Prepare fur boarding me ship. The morning breeze smells like a summer rose—a sweet honey rose! Today we sail into the wind."

Releasing the prisoners to fend for themselves on the deserted island, Captain John and his men shove off to find new victims of their raiding habits and secure the booty they have already captured.

He watches the small island shore fade away. Rubbing his black beard, he

ponders his raids in the Caribbean seas of wintertime and announces, "We've got to find a safe tree-lined island, like Abaco in the Caribbean, to bury our treasure."

They sail north. The waves slam against the boat.

Splash! Splatter! Splash!

They pass small islands.

"Got to find a safe place to bury the treasure," says Captain John from the deck. The waves swell as they turn northwest.

"Watch the wheel," barks the captain.

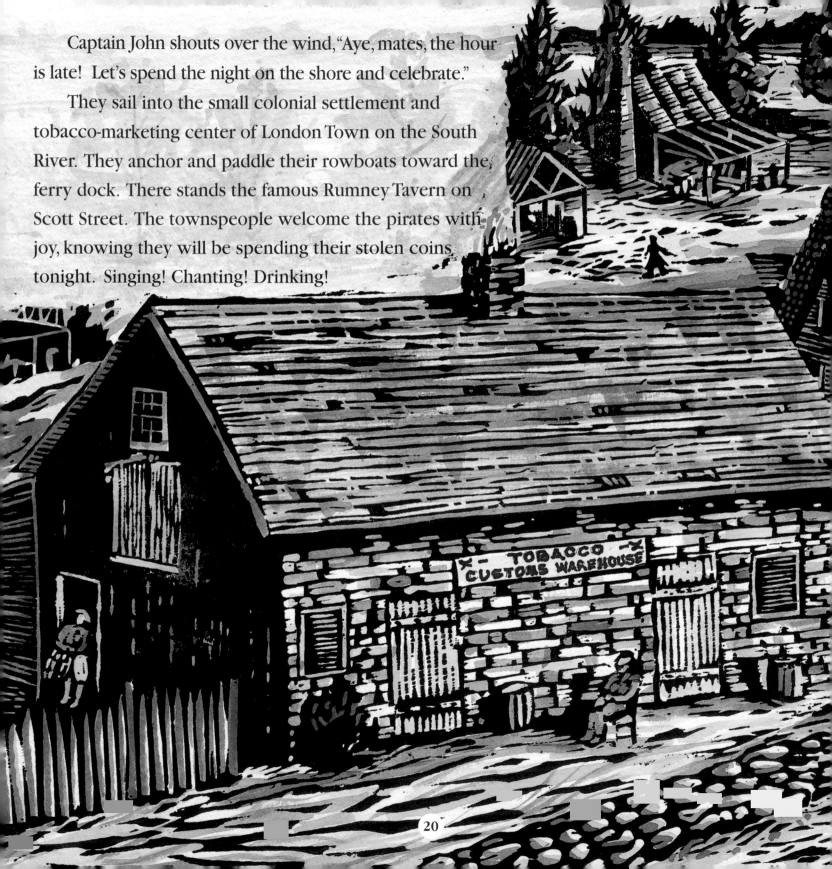

Captain John shouts over the wind, "Aye, mates, the hour is late! Let's spend the night on the shore and celebrate."

They sail into the small colonial settlement and tobacco-marketing center of London Town on the South River. They anchor and paddle their rowboats toward the ferry dock. There stands the famous Rumney Tavern on Scott Street. The townspeople welcome the pirates with joy, knowing they will be spending their stolen coins tonight. Singing! Chanting! Drinking!

TOBACCO CUSTOMS WAREHOUSE

Inside Rumney's Tavern, they spend their golden coins. Captain Bloodsworth pounds the table with his fist and shouts loudly, "Arrr! I will buy ye mates food and drink. Let's tip our blackjacks for our safe return to sea."

They drink rum and beer, gulp their food, and celebrate. Their bellies are full and they fall asleep—Snore! Snort! Snore!—in the tavern's rooms.

Awake by dawn, the captain and crew eat a hearty breakfast.

Then Captain John exclaims, "Aargh! Let's row to my ship, me hearties, we must leave London Town for the bay!"

The winds are calm. They sail eastward, leaving the craggy coastline behind, as the rhythmic waves spray surf into their faces.

"Avast, ye captain! The shore of that large island ahead is full of high pines. Aye, I guarantee ye, it is the ideal land," says a pirate, high on his perch. The captain and crew look on with excitement.

They sail towards the golden sandy shores of the island's southern point and drop anchor. "Mates, get the treasure into me rowboats," the captain commands.

The pirates load the rowboats and paddle to shore. Known to Captain Bloodsworth, small tribes of Native Americans called the Matapeakes and the Monoponsons live on Kent Island. They are friendly. Unknown to the captain, a warlike tribe of the dreaded Susquehannocks is camping on the island's thickly covered shores. "C'mere with me chests and follow me," commands Captain John.

They walk into the forest bearing the heavy trunks. Finding a sandy area, Captain John exclaims, "Aye, mates, this is where we will bury the treasure!"

The pirates keep guard and several mates dig two large holes.

"Aye, aye, a perfect place for the chests full of jewelry and coins," says Captain Bloodsworth. He draws a map of the treasure site and exclaims, "Aye! We shall return some day and collect our riches."

The pirates walk back through the thick cover of woods toward their boats. On the beach, a wild group of savage Susquehannocks shout, "Attack!"

A battle rages and many die. Red stains the sandy yellow beach.

The captain and several of his crew survive and escape onto a rowboat. Captain John commands, "Aargh! Row fast, mates, to me ship!"

Captain John, with his two remaining mates, climbs onto the ship and sets sail south toward Bloodsworth Island. They sail straight into the reddish-orange setting sun, but the captain never reaches Bloodsworth Island. The British prisoners' fates are unknown. Best of all, the two treasure chests are still buried on Kent Island's Bloody Point. Can you find them?

Aye! Let the search begin with your map and GPS. *(N 38 degrees 51 minutes latitude and W 76 degrees 22.4 minutes longitude.)* "Avast ye, mates. Shiver me timbers!"